Ashok Rajagopalan's main aim in life is to make people, especially little people, laugh. He has been doing this since 1989, by writing and illustrating picture books, chapter books, comics and magazine pages. He lives in a quiet part of Chennai with his family and books.

Other books in the series:

Gulgul in Sea-saw Gara

Gulgul in Parapara

The ADVENTURES of Gulgul

GULGUL IN JUNGALU

Ashok Rajagopalan

talking CUB

An Imprint of Speaking Tiger Books

TALKING CUB

Published by Speaking Tiger Books LLP
4381/4, Ansari Road, Daryaganj

New Delhi 110002

First published in paperback in Talking Cub
by Speaking Tiger Books in 2020

ISBN: 978-93-89958-96-6

10 9 8 7 6 5 4 3 2 1

The moral right of the author has been asserted.
Typeset in Crimson Text by Jojy Philip
Printed At: MP Printers (A unit of DB Corp. Ltd.) Noida 201305

To Sudeshna Shome Ghosh,

friend, philosopher and

editor of this series

Jungalu

'How far, Papa? How far, how far?' asked Gulgul.

'Hey, Gulgul, careful! Stop pushing me!' said Jit. He steered the space car through the rocks.

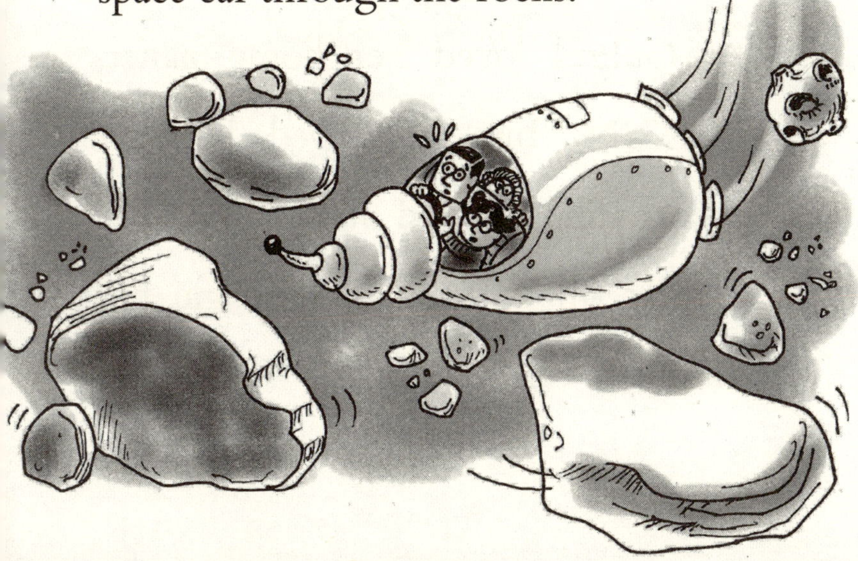

'Don't disturb your poor papa while he is driving, darling,' said Megha from the back. 'It is dangerous to disturb drivers.'

'Because you were in such a hurry,' said Jit, 'I took this shortcut. Big mistake!'

'But are we there yet?' asked Gulgul.

Gulgul loved her home-planet, GR33N. But she loved holidays more. She nagged and nagged her father till he took Gulgul and her mother on a holiday. They flew their space-car to H4H4H0, which was only a two-hour flight from home. The whole planet was an amusement park, and Gulgul spent two whole days roller-coasting, slip-sliding, tube-diving, squealing and screaming.

Finally, it was time to go home. Gulgul did not mind. She had begun to miss home now.

She had begun to miss her TV wall. She missed her collection of space-car toys. Most of all, she missed her pet robot-parrot Paru. So now they were in the space-car going back to GR33N.

'I miss home, Mamma! I miss my room!' she said.

'Your messy room,' reminded Megha.

'When will we reach home, Papa?' asked Gulgul shaking his arm. 'When, when, when?'

'Stop! Don't...HEY! See what you have done!' her father yelled.

THOCK! The car hit a rock.

THUCK! It bounced on another

rock. BOCK! And another. Rock after rock knocked on the car.

Phut...Phut... Phut...said the car.

'THE ENGINE IS HIT!' yelled Jit.

'Bad girl, Gulgul!' said Megha.

'Sorry!' said Gulgul.

Jit looked at the map screen.

'There's a planet nearby. It's called Jungalu. No, no...not Jungalu. JUN-

84-LU. We can land there for now,' he said.

'And I will help repair the car,' said Megha.

'But…but…but…' said Gulgul.

Phut…Phut…Phut…said the car, bouncing up and down.

The planet, first a small ball in the distance, came closer and closer.

'Trees, mountains and lakes,' said Megha. 'No buildings or streets. It's just a big jungle.'

'Wait. Let me steer the car to a lake,' said Jit. 'No need to worry now.'

Phut…phut…phut…tup, tup tup, POOOOOOSH.

'STOPPED! THE ENGINE HAS STOPPED!' said Jit.

'I miss Paru!' wailed Gulgul.

'Quiet, you pest! We are going to crash!' said Jit.

'Put on your helmet!' said Megha, putting hers on.

'Next time, please sit at the back,' said Jit. 'Let Mamma sit here.'

The space-car had stopped flying and started falling.

'There, that lake!' said Megha. 'Steer the thing to that big lake!'

'And please switch on the bubble,' said Jit.

As the space-car fell, Jit steered it towards the lake. They were falling very fast now.

SPLOSH! The space-car sank like a rock. Jit pressed a switch and the top opened. The three floated out of the car in a big bubble.

'This is fun!' said Gulgul.

'What do we do now?' asked Jit.

'Let's get out of the water first,' said Megha.

'EEEEEEEEEEEEEEEE!' screamed Gulgul.

'What?' asked Megha, 'AIEEEEEEE!'

'OOOOOOOOOOOOOH!' said Jit. 'Giant octopus! HELP!'

A long and spotted arm-like thing wrapped itself around the bubble.

BLURP! It pulled the bubble out of the water and up in the air.

'HELP!' shouted Jit.

'HELP!' yelled Megha.

'HELP! Let me go!' screamed Gulgul.

It let them go. The bubble whooshed through the air to land on a bush.

PLOCH! BLUB, BLUB, BLUB, it bounced on the ground. After it rolled to a stop, the three of them came out of the balloon safely. They felt giddy, but they were safe.

'It's okay,' said Megha, taking her helmet off and breathing deeply. 'We can breathe the air here.'

'Oh?' said Jit, 'Okay, then...RUN! It's coming out of the water!'

SLURP!

BLORP! The

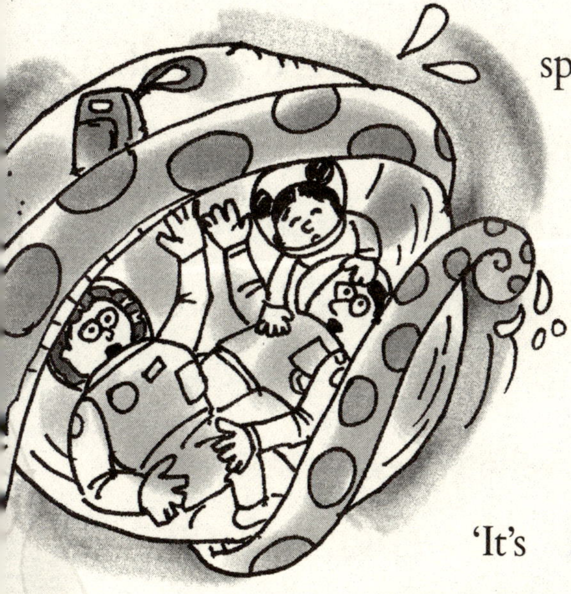

spotted arm came out, followed by a head and two tusks.

'It's a yellow elephant!' said Gulgul.

'Shouldn't we run for help?' asked Jit.

'It helped us out of the water,' said Megha, 'It's just an elephant. Helpful elephant.'

'Hungry elephant!' yelled Gulgul. 'It pulled us out to eat us up!'

The spotted creature came out of the lake. It looked like an elephant. It had ears and tusks like an elephant. But it was yellow. Yellow body with pink patches. The tusks were striped blue. And the trunk was about three times longer than an elephant's trunk. The trunk was what they had mistaken for an

octopus. The yellow elephant with pink patches, striped tusks and long trunk walked up to them and bowed its head.

'Elephant?' said the strange animal. 'What is an elephant?'

Hatch Patch

'You speak!' exclaimed Megha.

'Surely I speak,' said the strange animal. 'Some of us here don't squeak or speak, but I do.'

'How do you do?' asked Megha, 'I am Megha. This is Jit.'

'How do you do?' said Jit and pushed Gulgul forward. 'This is our daughter, Gulgul.'

'Hi,' said Gulgul. The stranger

shook hand and trunk with them.

'I am Hatch Patch,' he said. 'Welcome to our blue and green planet. Nice of you to "drop" in. You really dropped in!' He laughed at his own joke.

'Hatch Patch, ha, ha, ha!' laughed Gulgul. Her mother frowned.

'Don't laugh at somebody's name, Gulgul,' she said. 'It's rude.'

'Look at Hatch Patch, Mamma,' said Gulgul. 'He laughs, too!'

'Ha, ha, ha!' said Hatch Patch. 'Gulgul! What a sweet and funny name! Please follow me, people. I'll take you to my home.'

They followed Hatch Patch through the jungle to his home. He lived in a giant green house. The upper branches of four tall trees were plaited to form a high roof. Smaller trees made the walls. In it lived his happy family—two little boys and their mother.

'Welcome to our home,' said the mother, who had orange and blue skin. 'I am Match Patch. And these are Pitch Patch and Katch Patch.' Two little Patches peeped at the guests from behind their mother.

'These are Jit, Megha and Gulgul,' Hatch Patch introduced them to his family.

Jit and his family said hello and thank you. Gulgul did

not laugh. The little Patches were too cute to be laughed at. They didn't have tusks yet but had spots like their father. Pitch Patch was blue with yellow spots, and Katch Patch was pink with purple patches. Gulgul went forward to shake hand and trunk with the shy children.

Mamma Patch cooked them a grand feast of strange nuts, funny fruit and soft grass.

Gulgul did not like the grass much but ate it all up politely.

'Thank you for a nice lunch,

Aunty,' she told Match Patch. Megha smiled, proud of her polite daughter. She did not say it out aloud, but she wished her daughter was like that at home, too.

Pitch Patch and Katch Patch took Gulgul outside to play. The big people sat and talked inside the house.

'Do you go to school?' asked Gulgul.

'School?' asked Pitch Patch.

'What is school?' asked Katch Patch.

'Oh, just a place you go to, every day,' said Gulgul. 'Let's play Hide and Seek.'

'What is…' said Pitch Patch.

'I'll show you,' said Gulgul.

'Afterwards, we will show you how to play Mud or Stone,' said Katch Patch.

'Our phones are not working,' said Jit to Hatch Patch, 'So we can't call someone for help to return home.'

'What is a phone?' asked Hatch Patch.

'It's inside this,' said Jit showing Hatch Patch his helmet. 'I'll show you.'

Jit put on his helmet and said, 'Okay, Phone, call breakdown service.'

'Sorry, I cannot connect to the network,' said the phone.

'Okay, Phone, call my office.'

'Sorry, I cannot connect to the network,' said the phone.

'Nice and funny toy!' said Hatch Patch and laughed.

'It's not a toy, it's...' began Jit, but Megha interrupted him.

'Can you help us take our space-car out of the lake, please, Mister Hatch?' she asked. 'I am an engineer. I know how to repair it. If you can pull it out, it would be most helpful.'

'Yes, please,' said Jit.

'I am sorry, friends,' said Hatch Patch, 'but I cannot. You see, the lake is a bottomless lake.'

'Bottomless?' asked Jit and Megha together.

'Yes, bottomless. It's a long tunnel that stretches from one end of the planet to the other. There's a lake at the other end, too. Your space-car will be somewhere in the middle of our planet!'

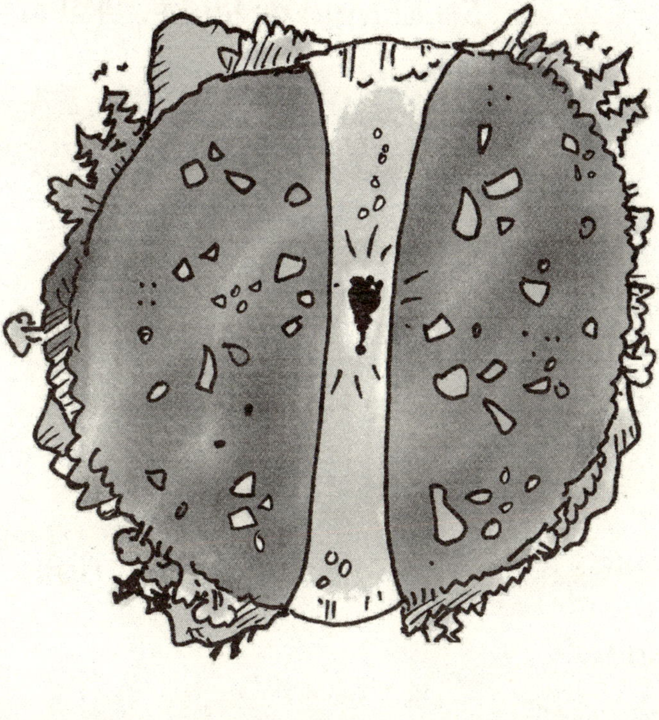

When Gulgul and the little Patches came inside, the house was silent. Jit looked worried. Megha was thinking deeply. Match Patch and Hatch Patch were in the kitchen.

'We played many games, Mamma. Hide and Seek, Mud or Stone...Papa, I want to ask you something,' said Gulgul. 'Can we stay here for a few days? I like it here.'

'We are stuck here forever!' said Jit. 'You can stay here for good!'

'What?' asked Gulgul. 'No, no! I miss home. I want to go home right now!'

'Quiet, please, you two,' said Megha. 'Let me think. I think I have a plan.'

The Zingjuck

Megha's plan was ready. Back home, Megha was an engineer and inventor. In fact, almost all the machines at home were made by Megha, not bought at a store.

'With some help, I can make a zingjuck,' said Megha to Jit and Gulgul.

'What's a zingjuck?' they asked.

'A zingjuck is a big platform,' Megha told them. 'It will throw our bubble out of the planet and into space. From there, we can phone for help. We will get good signal there. Then we can book a space-cab.'

Jit's face brightened like an electric bulb.

'Yay!' said Gulgul. 'But let's stay here a few days like I wanted.'

'It will take some time to build the zingjuck, anyway,' said Megha.

'Yay!' said Gulgul and danced

around the room with the two little Patches.

Megha opened her bag and took out her design pad. She began designing the zingjuck.

It took Megha a whole day to design. It would have taken others a month to do, but Megha was a genius inventor. Jit and Gulgul did not disturb her. They went out with Hatch Patch to explore. They helped Hatch Patch collect wood and leaves.

'We do not cut trees for firewood,' explained Hatch Patch. 'We collect old and dry branches, and little twigs, that have fallen down.' He picked up a big piece of wood, that was a 'little twig' to the big animal, but a long branch for a human.

'Oh! You mean that nobody in Jungalu cuts trees for wood?' asked Gulgul.

'Jungalu?'

'Your planet, Uncle,' said Gulgul.

'Oh! No, nobody cuts trees here. We leave things pretty much as they are. Fruits and nuts we pluck for food, of course.'

'What happens when people cut down trees, Uncle?' asked Gulgul. 'Is everybody good here? Nobody is bad?'

'Mind your manners, Gulgul!' said Jit, 'Don't ask rude questions!'

'Aww, Papa,' said Gulgul. 'I just wanted to find out, not being rude at all.'

Hatch Patch laughed.

'We did have bad and naughty people who tried to break branches of trees,' he said. 'Not anymore, we do not. No trouble now, at all! Ha, ha, ha!'

'What happened to them?' asked Gulgul.

'They were punished by the great and wise Mahali!' said Hatch Patch.

'Who's Manali?' asked Gulgul.

'Mahali,' Hatch Patch corrected Gulgul. 'Our wise and respected leader. We listen to her because she is wise and respected. I shall take you to meet her tomorrow. We have not had visitors for more than ten years! Mahali likes to know everything that happens here. All the news, the newer news the better, ha ha ha!'

With a good collection of wood and leaves, they returned home.

'You can sit on my back if you are

tired,' said Hatch Patch. 'I can carry you.'

On Gulgul's home planet, GR33N, people were not allowed to ride on animals. It was against the law.

'We are not allowed to sit on animals...others...back home,' said Gulgul.

'What about children?' asked Hatch. 'Cannot parents carry their children?'

'Oh, that's different,' said Jit. 'We used to carry Gulgul around when she was a baby.'

Hatch Patch laughed.

'Then hop on to my back,' he said. 'You two are as small as children to me. Smaller than my children, actually, ha, ha, ha!' With his trunk, he lifted them up and put them on his back, with their bundles of wood.

By the time they reached home, Megha was ready with the design for the zingjuck. She showed them the 3D drawing proudly.

'Yay!' said Megha.

'Very pretty,' said Match Patch.

'Now, Mister Hatch Patch, please help us. We need some steel and wood,' said Megha.

'Oh,' said Hatch Patch and looked at Match sadly.

'I am sorry,' said Match Patch, 'We are sorry. Nobody is allowed to cut down trees for wood or dig for metals here. You can take these pieces of wood, if you want.'

'These will not do! I need bigger pieces. And I need steel to make tools to make the thing. I need screw drivers and saws and whatnot! How will we leave the planet now?'

'What will we do now?' said Jit.

The Patches looked at Gulgul

and her worried family. They felt bad for these sad people.

Wise Mahali

'Let us go to Mahali,' said Hatch Patch, the next morning, after breakfast.

'I don't feel like going anywhere,' said Megha, 'till I know what to do.'

'Mahali is our wise leader,' said Match Patch. 'She will know what to do.'

'Yes, that is right,' added Hatch

Patch. 'Anyway, I have to tell her about your visit.'

'Oh, come along, Mamma,' said Gulgul. 'She could tell us what to do.'

'And bring along your design, Megha,' said Jit.

Both families left for Mahali's house, which was on a hill, far away. Match Patch and Hatch Patch carried the humans on their backs, while Pitch Patch and Katch Patch walked.

'Wonder what colour their leader

is,' said Gulgul to Megha. 'I hope she is green. It will be nice to see a green elephant.'

'Hush, darling,' said her mother. 'Don't say things like that.'

They climbed the hill and after a while, reached the top. The top was flat, with a big and dark hole in the centre.

'Like a volcano!' said Gulgul.

'This is where our wise leader lives,' said Match Patch.

'Careful, everybody,' warned Hatch Patch. 'Do not go too close to the edge. You may fall inside! Though Mahali will be happy you dropped in! Ha, ha, ha!'

'Don't laugh loudly, Hatch!' said Match Patch. 'I think I hear our leader coming.'

'Sorry,' said Hatch Patch. There was a scratching noise from the hole.

Gulgul peeped into the hole. She was eager to know what Mahali looked like. The noise grew louder, and finally Mahali came out of her hole.

Mahali was not a green elephant. She did not even look like an elephant. She was a mouse. A mouse that was as big as a house. A human house, that is, not a Patch house.

Her whiskers, as thick and long as bamboo sticks, were seen first. Then came a big brown nose. Next were seen the great head and ears. Finally, Mahali came out of the hole

completely. She looked down at the four Patches, and the three humans. She kept looking at them for a whole minute without speaking.

Finally, after what seemed to Gulgul a very long time, the great mouse spoke.

'Squeak!' she said.

'Does she only squeak?' asked Gulgul.

'No, no, Gulgul,' said Match Patch, 'she is asking us to speak. Even when we speak loudly, it is just a squeak to her.'

'Greetings, Wise Leader,' said Hatch Patch.

'Oh, I see,' said Gulgul, 'that is why when mice are speaking to each other, it sounds like squeaking to us!'

'Hush, darling,' said Megha.

'Let's hear what their leader has to say.'

'Greetings to you all,' said Mahali. 'Now, squeak. Who are these new people?'

'They are our guests from another planet, Wise Mahali,' said Hatch Patch. 'Their car fell into our bottomless lake. I saved them and took them home.'

'Good of you, Hatch Patch,' said Mahali.

'Thank you, Mahali,' said Hatch Patch. 'Nice of you to say that.'

'They wish to return to their planet, Wise Leader,' Match Patch informed Mahali.

'They need our help,' added Hatch Patch.

'Yes, please, Wise Mouse,' said Megha.

'What is a mouse?' asked Mahali.

'Please, Wise Leader,' said Megha, 'I hear that we are not allowed to cut wood or mine for metal in Jungalu.'

'What is Jungalu?' asked Mahali.

'That is the nice name they have given our planet,' said Hatch Patch.

'That's good of you, guests. It is a nice and funny name,' said Mahali. 'What do you want from Mahali?'

'Please allow us to cut wood and mine metal,' said Megha, 'so I can build a zingjuck, a machine that will help us return home.' She took out her pad and showed the design. She explained how it would throw their bubble into space.

'That's clever of you. But Mahali is sorry, Guest,' said Mahali. 'Mahali cannot change our laws. We cannot allow you to cut wood or dig for metal.'

'Then we are stuck here forever!' said Jit.

Four Longfellows

Mahali was silent for a long time. Then she spoke.

'Do not worry, guests,' she said. 'Mahali will think deeply and tell you what to do.'

Then Mahali closed her eyes.

'Has she gone to sleep?' asked Gulgul after some time.

'Hush, darling,' said Megha.

Finally, the big mouse opened her eyes.

'Mahali will help you,' she said. 'For that you will need some helpers to help you. Bring them here.

'They are:

Four Longfellows

One Bluglug

Eight Flippots

One Buzzby

One Groffy

Two Flooklums

One Kluplet

One Pikquick

One Heekeek

'After you bring them here,

Mahali will tell you what to do.'

After saying this, Mahali went into her big hole.

'Bluglug! Flooklum! Ha, ha, ha!' said Gulgul.

'I can't make head or tail of this,' said Jit. 'Longfellow? Flippot?'

'All have heads. Some have tails,' said Hatch Patch. 'Come, let us bring them here. We will help you.'

'We have to go to the

other side of the planet for some of them,' said Match Patch.

'Oh, won't that take many days?' asked Megha.

'If we start now, it will take us only nine days. One day for each on our list,' said Hatch. 'Luckily, our planet is a small planet.'

'Nine days? That is too long!' said Jit. 'We have so much work to do back home! Megha can't take leave! Gulgul has school!'

'And our phones will be low on battery!' said Megha.

'Papa,' said Gulgul, 'let's split into three groups and find three helpers each. Three times three is nine. It will take us only three days.'

'Clever girl, Gulgul!' said Jit, proudly.

'I will bring the first three on the list,' said Gulgul. 'Four longfellows, one bluglug and eight flippots. Mamma and you can divide the rest among yourselves, as you like.'

'That sounds fine, Gulgul,' said Jit. 'Good luck, take care.'

'I will come with you, Gulgul,'

said Hatch Patch. 'What a sweet and funny name, ha ha!'

'Thank you, Uncle,' said Gulgul, though she did not like him laughing every time he said her name.

'Come, let us go look for some longfellows, then!' said Hatch Patch. He set off, with Gulgul on his back.

'I wonder what longfellows look like,' thought Gulgul. 'Maybe they are some kind of giraffe.'

It was evening when they reached the river near which the longfellows lived. Hatch Patch plucked some fruit from the super-tall trees there for them to eat. Then they drank the river water.

'There!' said Hatch Patch suddenly. 'Look at the top of that tree!'

A horned head, much like a giraffe's, peeped out from a high branch of a tall tree.

'How tall this longfellow must be!' said Gulgul. 'Taller than a giraffe, I think!'

'They are not tall people,' said Hatch Patch. 'Hey, Mister Longfellow, please come down and talk to us.'

The longfellow was not tall, just as Hatch had said. Its neck was short, but the body was very long. It climbed down, twisting and turning around the trunk of the tree like a snake. It was coloured like a giraffe, though. It was yellow with brown spots.

'What do you want, Mister Patch?' it asked. 'My name is Thooky. And who is this? Never seen someone like this before!'

'Not me, our Wise Leader wants you,' said Hatch. 'This is Gulgul, our guest from another planet.'

'What a funny name, ha ha,' said Thooky. Gulgul who had stopped herself from laughing with great difficulty, grew angry.

'Not as funny as Thooky!' she said.

'Oh, thank you, Gulgul!' said Thooky. Gulgul did not know what to say to that!

'We need three more of your friends, Thooky,' said Hatch. 'Mahali said she wanted four longfellows.'

'Oh, that will be easy. What an honour to be called by Mahali! Let me go call Fooky, Sooky and Cooky.'

Gulgul burst out laughing.

Lug the Bluglug

Thooky promised to go to Mahali's place as soon as he could gather his friends. Hatch Patch and Gulgul set off. They had to meet the bluglug.

'We have to go down the river,' said Hatch Patch. 'There is a small and round island where the river grows wider. A bluglug lives on that island.'

'Wonder what bluglugs look like,' thought Gulgul. 'Sounds like somebody who drinks a lot of water. Is it a frog? A snail?'

It was night when they came to where the river became very wide. Just as Hatch had said, there was a small and round island in the middle of the river.

'Let us wait till morning,' said Hatch. 'That is when bluglugs come out of the river.'

'Okay, Uncle,' said Gulgul, lying down on Hatch Patch's back. 'Please wake me up when needed.'

'SNORE!' replied Hatch Patch, who always slept standing up. 'SNOH-OH-OH-ORE!'

Hatch Patch and Gulgul had fruits and nuts for breakfast. Hatch Patch had also brought a bunch of fresh grass to eat. Gulgul said she did not want any grass; she was full. After breakfast, Hatch Patch took her to the round island. It was a rocky island without plants or trees, just stones.

'What a boring island!' said Gulgul. She sat down on a rock and waited, hands on cheeks. Hatch walked around the island. After a long time, Hatch gave a shout.

'Here comes a bluglug!' he said, pointing to the river with his trunk. Gulgul stood up to see better.

'Gluggings, Glugs! I am Lug,' said the bluglug, splashing out of the water. He was a fat fish with a big fan-like tail.

'Gluggings?' asked Gulgul.

'He means "greetings", Gulgul,'

explained Hatch Patch. He turned to the bluglug.

'Greetings, Lug! I am Hatch Patch,' said Hatch Patch.

'Hi!' said Gulgul. 'I am Gulgul.'

'What can I gloo for you, Hatch Patch and Glug Glug?' asked Lug.

'Gulgul,' said Gulgul, frowning.

'The wise Mahali wants to see

you, Lug,' said Hatch Patch. 'As soon as possible.'

'That is glood! Very glood! I will glo there right away!' said Lug. He leapt into the river and disappeared.

'He travels faster by water than land. He will swim down the river and then go up the hill,' said Hatch Patch.

'He can breathe in the water and out of it, too?' asked Gulgul.

'Sure,' said Hatch Patch. With Gulgul on his back, he waded towards the riverbank.

'Now for the flippots!' shouted Gulgul. 'What fun! I didn't know that finding these helpers would be so easy!'

'You know, Gulgul,' said Hatch Patch, 'Longfellows and bluglugs are easy to speak to. But talking to flippots is difficult. Making them understand is hard.'

'How hard?' asked Gulgul.

'You will see,' said Hatch Patch. He pointed to the distance, to the beach where the river joined the sea.

'We will find them there,' he

said. 'We have to take them gifts. Something to eat. Will you wait here while I go get some yayapas?'

'Yayapas?'

'Yes, and some nanabas.'

He returned with the promised fruit. Yayapas were pink papayas. Nanabas were blue bananas.

The beach had sand of a pale purple colour. Hatch Patch put the fruit down, on the sand.

'Yay!' said Gulgul, running towards the sea.

'Hey!' said Hatch Patch. 'Not so loud! You will scare the flippots away.'

'Oh, okay. Look at those pretty seagulls,' said Gulgul, pointing

towards the sky. 'How they fly! Up and down, left and right!'

'They are not called seagulls,' said Hatch Patch. 'They are flippots.'

Eight Flippots

'Take a fruit and wave it about,' said Hatch Patch.

'Why, Uncle?' asked Gulgul.

'To attract the flippots, of course,' said Hatch Patch. 'It will bring them here. They love fruit.'

Gulgul grabbed a yayapa and waved it about.

Swoop! Whoosh! Hatch Patch was right!

Two flippots landed before Gulgul and Hatch Patch.

'Wow! Cool!' said Gulgul.

The flippots were winged hippos. They were blue with yellow stripes. Their wings were like glass, and looked like dragonfly wings. Each wing was as long as Gulgul herself.

'Twee! Pwee!' said one.

'Chwee!' said the other. Gulgul pushed the bunches of fruit towards them. With happy cries, they began

eating the fruits as fast as they could.

After finishing the fruits, they looked at Gulgul for more. More flippots from the sky came flying down but flew away again.

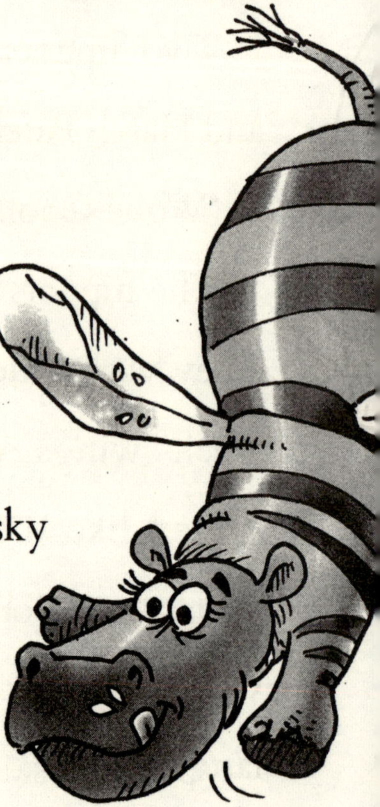

'Mahali wants you,' said Hatch Patch.

'Mwee?' asked the first flippot.

'We need eight of them,' said Hatch Patch to Gulgul. 'Keep talking to them. I will be back with more fruit.' Hatch Patch left.

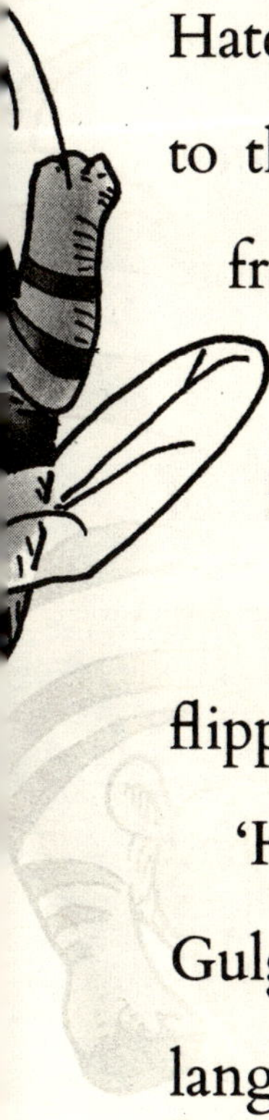

'Hi,' said Gulgul to her new friends, 'I am Gulgul!'

'Gwee?' said the second flippot.

'How can I talk to you?' asked Gulgul. 'We don't know each other's language!'

'Pwee wee,' said the first flippot.

They looked about for more

fruit. Not finding any, they turned to leave.

'Hey! Please don't go,' said Gulgul to their fat backs, 'Uncle Hatch is bringing you more nanabas!'

They turned at the sound of 'nanabas'. They understood that, it seemed. Luckily, before the flippots went, Hatch Patch returned. He had three big bunches of nanabas this time. He waved the bunches in the air. More flippots came flying down then.

'One, two, three, four, five,' said Gulgul. 'There comes one more. Six! Six plus two is eight! We have eight flippots!'

Hatch Patch gave the eight flippots two bunches of nanabas to eat. They finished it in no time.

'Okay, time to go,' he said. He put Gulgul and the remaining nanabas on his back.

'But will they follow us?' asked Gulgul.

'They will follow the fruit, ha ha,' said Hatch Patch and began walking.

The flippots followed, making all kinds of noises. They flew around Hatch Patch, hoping to be given some nanabas.

'That's not very kind,' said Gulgul.

'That's the only way,' said Hatch. 'We are going to give this bunch to that bunch anyway, ha ha.'

Gulgul did not laugh. She did not like to cheat the poor animals.

'Do not worry,' said Hatch Patch. 'I will give them lots of fruit to eat once they come to Mahali's hole.'

They went in a long line. First walked Hatch Patch with Gulgul on his back. Then followed the flippots one by one, flying behind them, buzzing and tweeting. Now and then they made their funny noises.

'I guess what I speak sounds like funny noises to them, too,' said Gulgul.

'Yes,' said Hatch Patch, 'It is their language.'

'But how will they help?' asked Gulgul, 'They don't understand us. We don't understand them!'

'The wise Mahali will know how to talk to them, I think. She knows everything,' said Hatch Patch.

On the way, Gulgul saw some big and round fruit hanging from a tall tree.

'What fruit is that?' she asked Hatch Patch.

'Matterwellons,' said Hatch Patch.

'Can you reach them?' Gulgul asked.

'Of course,' said Hatch Patch proudly. 'My trunk can reach the top of the tallest trees on the planet!'

'Then please get some,' said Gulgul. 'I am hungry, and the flippots can eat, too.'

'The flippots can eat anyway, anytime! Ha ha ha! Fine, I will get some matterwellons.'

Hatch Patch unrolled his trunk and plucked a few matterwellons.

Thop! Thop! Thop! Thop! They

dropped to the ground. The flippots flew down like big bees buzzing to a flower full of honey. Slurp! Blurp! They ate up all the delicious fruit with shouts of delight.

Gulgul lay on Hatch Patch's back. She was happy now. She had eaten a piece of matterwellon. That was not the reason why she was happy, though. She did not feel bad now. She was happy that they

could give the flippots something more to eat.

She closed her eyes. She slept with a smile on her lips.

Back to Mahali's Hole

It was morning when Gulgul, Hatch Patch and the flippots reached Mahali's home.

'Oh! Coooooooool!' said Gulgul.

Quite a noisy crowd was gathered around the hole. Gulgul stared at the other helpers on the list standing beside Jit and Megha.

'Funny-looking animals,' she thought. Jit and Megha looked

tired, but proud. Match Patch and the little Patches were there, too. All were waiting for the wise Mahali to come out of her hole. She waved to her family and the Patch's. She then went around thanking the helpers for coming. She shook hand and paw with Thooky and was introduced to Fooky, Sooky and Cooky.

'All of you look like Thooky!' she said.

'Hush, darling,' said Megha. 'That's not a nice thing to say.'

Gulgul went over to Lug, who had dragged himself up the hill with great difficulty. He was still huffing and puffing.

'Thank you very much, Lug,' she said. 'Must have been tough, climbing this hill.'

'It is fine,' said Lug, 'It is an honour to meet Mahali.'

'Did you find it tough getting the helpers to come, Gulgul?' asked Jit.

'We had some difficulty getting the flippots to come. But Uncle

Hatch knew what to do,' said Gulgul. She pointed to the eight flippots, who were busy eating up the nanabas.

'Okay, let me go see the others,' said Gulgul. 'What fun!' She skipped away to greet the helpers. They seemed to have the funniest names. And they seemed to make a lot of noise.

'Here comes Mahali!' All the noise stopped.

'We can hear a pin drop!' said Gulgul.

'Hush,' said Megha.

Mahali came out of the hole. She looked around. She smiled at each and everyone in the crowd.

'Greetings, everyone!' she said.

'Greetings, Wise Mahali!' said everyone. Mahali looked around again. She smiled again.

'Mahali is happy to see that everyone on the list is here,' she said, 'Proud of you all. Thank you for coming. Megha, come forward, please.'

Megha went forward.

'Mahali will tell you how the helpers can help,' said Mahali. 'Show us the design again please.'

Megha showed her the design on her pad.

'Please give Mahali the pad,' said Mahali. Megha gave her the pad. Mahali looked at the design and shook her head.

'Once your bubble is up there, how will you get help? How will you steer the bubble?'

'I will call for help once up there,' said Megha. 'That was the plan.'

'Mahali will make a design now,' said Mahali. With Megha's help, Mahali made the design quickly.

'There!' said Mahali. 'Come here,

Hatch.' Mahali told Hatch Patch what to do.

'Hatch will tell the helpers what to do. They are here to help your bubble leave the planet,' said Mahali.

'How will the helpers help our bubble be zingjucked, Wise Mahali?' asked Gulgul.

'Good of you to ask, Gulgul,' said Mahali. 'Good luck to you all! Goodbye!'

Mahali went into her hole.

'How annoying! She didn't answer my question,' said Gulgul.

'No, but she told me what to do,' said Hatch Patch. 'I will take care of things. Do not worry.'

Hatch Patch went over to Thooky and his friends.

'The wise Mahali told me that you speak the language of the flippots,' Hatch Patch said.

'That is right,' said Thooky.

'Then please tell them to make a square shape,' said Hatch Patch.

Thooky spoke to the flippots. The eight flippots soon stood in the shape of a square.

'Why are they standing like that?' asked Jit.

'Let's wait and see,' said Megha. Hatch gave more orders to Thooky.

The four longfellows twisted like ropes and tied themselves around the eight flippots.

'I know, Mamma!' said Gulgul. 'See! They are making your zingjuck!'

Zing!

Soon, the zingjuck was ready. All the helpers had joined together to make the machine.

'This zingjuck looks like a jungzick,' laughed Gulgul. 'But it looks like fun, too!'

Hatch Patch returned to them with a proud smile.

'We are ready,' he said. 'You may enter the bubble. The other helpers will take care of everything.'

'Can we even steer the thing?' asked Megha.

'Sure you can,' said Hatch Patch. 'The bluglug with his big tail will help do that. If he turns his tail to the right, the zingjuck will move to the left. Tail to left, zingjuck to right.'

'Right!' said Jit.

'Ha ha,' laughed Hatch Patch. 'Now please enter the bubble, my friends.'

Gulgul and her parents said goodbye to the Patches.

'Please come again,' said Match

Patch. 'I will cook your favourite grass for you.'

'Yuck...I mean...thank you, Aunty. Bye, Aunty,' said Gulgul.

The two little Patches hugged Gulgul with their trunks.

'Bye, Katch! Bye, Pitch! I will miss you two,' said Gulgul.

'Bye, Gulgul,' said the little Patches. 'We will miss you too.'

'Bye, Uncle Hatch,' said Gulgul. 'Thank you for everything.'

'You are welcome,' said Hatch Patch. 'You are always welcome here! Farewell!'

The three put on their helmets and got into the bubble. Hatch Patch picked it up with his trunk. He placed the bubble in the centre of the zingjuck.

'Now what?' asked Gulgul.

'Wait, darling,' said Megha. 'Hatch knows what to do.'

Hatch said something to Thooky. Thooky spoke to the flippots.

'Chweepee, hwee, swee,' he said.

'Kwee, kwee,' said the flippots. The flippots flapped their wings. Slowly the zingjuck rose in the air.

'Yay!' said Gulgul.

The little Patches waved their trunks. Gulgul and her parents waved back.

The zingjuck did not go up much. Lug moved his tail. They now moved sideways.

'Where are they going?' asked Jit.

'Let's wait and see,' said Megha.

The flippots flew them all to Hatch Patch. Hatch Patch and Match Patch had tied their trunks together. They caught the zingjuck and began swinging it up and down. Up and down they went in the air. Gulgul felt quite giddy but she laughed. This was like one of the rides in H4H4H0.

'Whee!' she said. 'What fun!'

'What's he doing?' asked Jit. The Patches suddenly bowled it into the air.

'AIEEEEEEEEEEEEEEE!'

ZING!

shouted Jit.

'OOOOOOOOOOOOH!' shouted Megha.

'EEEEEEEEEEEEEEEE' yelled Gulgul. The bubble and zingjuck zoomed across the sky.

'HAAAAAAAAAAAAALP!' they screamed together.

Help!

The humans were still screaming when the zingjuck was high up in the sky. Then it began to fall. Thooky spoke to the flippots who flapped their wings again. The

zingjuck stopped falling. It flew gently over the clouds.

Megha stopped screaming first.

'Call Space-cab!' she said to her phone.

'Sorry, I cannot connect to the network,' said the phone.

'Oh, help!' said Jit.

'Bawwww!' cried Gulgul, 'I want to go home!'

'Wait, darling,' said Megha, 'We are flying higher. We will get a signal anytime now. Please wait a bit.'

'Now we know why the Patches swung us up and down,' said Jit. 'To throw us up in the sky.'

'Yes,' said Megha. 'If he hadn't thrown us that far, the flippots would have had to fly that high. They would have been tired, poor things.'

'The wise mouse thought of everything,' said Jit.

'I am connected,' said the phone.

'Yay!' said Gulgul.

'Yay!' said Jit.

'Call Space-cab,' said Megha.

'Calling Space-cab,' said the phone.

Soon, a cab came to get them. The driver was surprised to see the strange collection of animals.

'Who called?' he asked. 'Whom should I pick up?'

'Us!' said Gulgul. Gulgul and her parents got out of the bubble. They got into the cab. They waved goodbye to the buzzby and the helpers. Some of the helpers waved back.

'Bwee, bwee!' said the flippots.

'Whew! What a welcome sight!' said Jit as they saw GR33N in the sky.

'Yay!' said Gulgul, 'Home!'

The cab dropped them home in no time.

Gulgul dashed into the house to see her robot parrot.

'Paru! I am home!'

'Welcome back, Gulgul!' said Paru.

Megha went straight to bed.

'Jit, your turn to cook today,' she said.

'Hey! I am tired, too!' he said, lying down on the couch. He switched on the TV wall.

'Let's order pizza, then,' said Megha.

Pizza tasted yummier after days of soft grass and funny fruit.

'Yum! You know, Mamma,' said Gulgul. 'I missed home when we were in Jungalu, but ...'

'It was still fun?' asked Megha.

'Yes, Mamma, it was fun,' said Gulgul. 'We should go to new planets again.'

'Next time, we will,' said Megha. 'What do you say, Jit?'

'Okay, but you should drive, and Gulgul must sit at the back,' said Jit.

'Yes,' said Megha, 'We can't keep buying a new car after each and every trip.'

'Aww, Mamma,' said Gulgul. She spoke to the TV wall.

'Wall, open Maps,' she said.

'Opening Maps,' said the TV wall.

The wall was now a map of hundreds of planets and stars.

'Where can we go next?' wondered Gulgul.

ALSO IN THIS SERIES BY ASHOK RAJAGOPALAN

GULGUL IN SEA-SAW GARA

In the sea, riding the waves was a fleet of five animals that were half-horse and half-fish.
'They are striped,' said Gulgul. 'They are not sea horses. They are seabras!'

Gulgul, along with her parents Megha and Jit, have gone to the planet C-54G4R4, or Sea-saw Gara. The whole planet is a like a giant waterpark. When Gulgul goes on a submarine ride, the submarine loses its way in the planet's waters! Soon they are rescued by giant octopuses who live in Octopus City. Here everyone lives in aquariums and eats sea-fruits, sea-nuts, seagrass, and even drinks seawater!

How will Gulgul and the other humans survive? Will they be able to find their way back to the waterpark? What will happen if the fierce half-fish and half-lion merlions attack?

Laugh out loud as Gulgul once again proves that with a little bit of luck and lots of clever ideas, there are amazing adventures waiting on every planet! Ashok Rajagopalan, creator of the bestselling Gajapati Kulapati books, brings his trademark wacky humour to a new series filled with adventure, friendship and fun.

ALSO IN THIS SERIES BY ASHOK RAJAGOPALAN

GULGUL IN PARAPARA

'What's a keypock?' asked Gulgul.
'It's like a peacock,' said Dinny. 'But its feathers change colours. All the colours of the rainbow, one by one.'

Dinny, Gulgul's cousin, loves collecting bird feathers. When Gulgul visits Dinny, her Aunt Jinny decides to take them to the planet P4R4P4R4 (Parapara) to find some rare keypock feathers. But wherever Gulgul goes, there is sure to be a super exciting adventure!

Parapara is a collection of many small planets and moons on which live birds of all shapes and sizes. When they land on Greenpara, they meet the bird Win King, and her three children Coo King, Thin King and Blin King who tell them where to find keypocks. But on the way, they are kidnapped by giant parrots as big as horses.

Will they be able to escape? Who will come to their rescue? Will Jinny, Dinny and Gulgul find a way to get back home with their feathers intact?

Ashok Rajagopalan, creator of the bestselling Gajapati Kulapati books, brings his trademark wacky humour to a new series filled with adventure, friendship and fun. Filled with funny birds and an even funnier aunt, the third book in The Adventures of Gulgul series will have you tweeting and squawking and hooting with laughter!